Marley is so excited to join the band.
She walks in and sees all of the shiny
instruments around the room.

Then, towards the back of the room she sees the drums.

Before class starts she sits and starts to bang on the drums with the sticks. BOOM, CRASH, SLAM! Marley like this very much.

When music class starts, the teacher instructs the students to start playing.

All of the band students begin to play the music together.

They are able to play together because they are reading the music that is in front of them.

Marley looks around confused not quite sure what to do. She starts to bang on the drums again. BOOM, CRASH, SLAM!

The students stop playing and they all look at Marley.
Marley is confused and a little embarrassed.
She does not understand why what she is playing
does not sound good with the rest of the class.

Marley sits quietly and listens for the rest of music class with the drumsticks in her lap.

After class, the teacher explains that if she practices the drums she will be able to play along with the music the class is playing.

Determined, Marley spends every free minute she has practicing the drums for next week's music class.

She plays before school.

She plays after school.

She even plays at night!

The next week in music class the teacher instructs the students to start playing again.

Marley is so excited; she has been waiting for
this moment all week!

The class starts playing.

Marley anxiously waits for her cue to start playing.

Her cue comes and she starts to play.

Marley is playing along with the class perfectly!
Marley is playing with the biggest smile on her face.
The teacher sees Marley and smiles with her.

When the song is over the teacher awards
Marley with Star Student of the week because
of her practice and dedication.

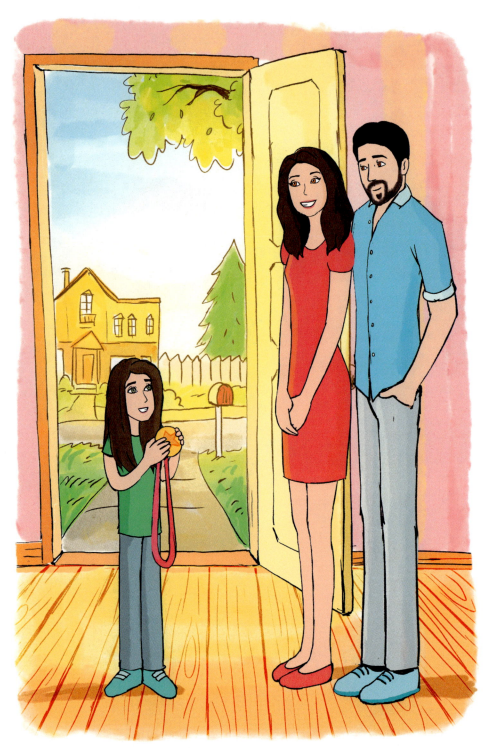

Marley rushes home after school to tell her mom and dad about her Star Student Award.

"We are so proud of you!"
Marley's parents tell her.

She turns and runs up to her room.

"Where are you going Marley?" her mom asks

"TO PRACTICE" Marley exclaims back.

Made in the USA
Monee, IL
14 July 2020

36488485R00017